The Stranger: A Drama

The Stranger: A Drama, in Five Acts

by August von Kotzebue

Copyright © 10/21/2015
Jefferson Publication

ISBN-13: 978-1518718694

Printed in the United States of America

All rights reserved. No part of this book may be reprinted or reproduced or utilized in any form or by any electronic, mechanical, or other means, now known or hereafter invented, including photocopying and recording, or in any form of storage or retrieval system, without prior permission in writing from the publisher.'

Table of Contents

ACT THE FIRST. 3
    SCENE I. 3
    SCENE II. 15
ACT THE SECOND. 21
    SCENE I. 21
    SCENE II. 28
    SCENE III. 31
    SCENE IV. 37
ACT THE THIRD. 38
    SCENE I. 38
    SCENE II. 48
ACT THE FOURTH. 53
    SCENE I. 53
    SCENE II. 62
ACT THE FIFTH. 69
    SCENE I. 69
    SCENE II. 71

ACT THE FIRST.

SCENE I.

The Skirts of Count Wintersen's *Park.—The Park Gates in the centre.—On one side a low Lodge, among the Trees.—On the other, in the back ground, a Peasant's Hut.*

Enter Peter.

Pet. Pooh! pooh!—never tell me.—I'm a clever lad, for all father's crying out every minute, "Peter," and "stupid Peter!" But I say, Peter is not stupid, though father will always be so wise. First, I talk too much; then I talk too little; and if I talk a bit to myself, he calls me a driveller. Now, I like best to talk to myself; for I never contradict myself, and I don't laugh at myself, as other folks do.

That laughing is often a plaguy teazing custom. To be sure, when Mrs. Haller laughs, one can bear it well enough; there is a sweetness even in her reproof, that somehow—But, lud! I had near forgot what I was sent about.—Yes, then they would have laughed at me indeed.—[*Draws a green purse from his pocket.*]—I am to carry this money to old Tobias; and Mrs. Haller said I must be sure not to blab, or say that she had sent it. Well, well, she may be easy for that matter; not a word shall drop from my lips. Mrs. Haller is charming, but silly, if father is right; for father says, "He, that spends his money is not wise," but "he that gives it away, is stark mad."

Enter the Stranger, *from the Lodge, followed by* Francis.—*At sight of* Peter, *the* Stranger *stops, and looks suspiciously at him.* Peter *stands opposite to him, with his mouth wide open. At length he takes off his hat, scrapes a bow, and goes into the Hut.*

Stra. Who is that?

Fra. The steward's son.

Stra. Of the Castle?

Fra. Yes.

Stra. [*After a pause.*] You were—you were speaking last night—

Fra. Of the old countryman?

Stra. Ay.

Fra. You would not hear me out.

Stra. Proceed.

Fra. He is poor.

Stra. Who told you so?

Fra. Himself.

Stra. [*With acrimony.*] Ay, ay; he knows how to tell his story, no doubt.

Fra. And to impose, you think?

Stra. Right!

Fra. This man does not.

Stra. Fool!

Fra. A feeling fool is better than a cold sceptic.

Stra. False!

Fra. Charity begets gratitude.

Stra. False!

Fra. And blesses the giver more than the receiver.

Stra. True.

Fra. Well, sir. This countryman—

Stra. Has he complained to you?

Fra. Yes.

Stra. He, who is really unhappy, never complains. [*Pauses.*] Francis, you have had means of education beyond your lot in life, and hence you are encouraged to attempt imposing on me:—but go on.

Fra. His only son has been taken from him.

Stra. Taken from him?

Fra. By the exigency of the times, for a soldier.

Stra. Ay!

Fra. The old man is poor.—

Stra. 'Tis likely.

Fra. Sick and forsaken.

Stra. I cannot help him.

Fra. Yes.

Stra. How?

Fra. By money. He may buy his son's release.

Stra. I'll see him myself.

Fra. Do so.

Stra. But if he is an impostor!

Fra. He is not.

Stra. In that hut?

Fra. In that hut. [Stranger *goes into the Hut.*] A good master, though one almost loses the use of speech by living with him. A man kind and clear—though I cannot understand him. He rails against the whole world, and yet no beggar leaves his door unsatisfied. I have now lived three years with him, and yet I know not who he is. A hater of society, no doubt; but not by Providence intended to be so. Misanthropy in his head, not in his heart.

Enter the Stranger *and* Peter, *from the Hut.*

Pet. Pray walk on.

Stra. [*To* Francis.] Fool!

Fra. So soon returned!

Stra. What should I do there?

Fra. Did you not find it as I said?

Stra. This lad I found.

Fra. What has he to do with your charity?

Stra. The old man and he understand each other perfectly well.

Fra. How?

Stra. What were this boy and the countryman doing?

Fra. [*Smiling, and shaking his head.*] Well, you shall hear. [*To* Peter.] Young man, what were you doing in that hut?

Pet. Doing!—Nothing.

Fra. Well, but you couldn't go there for nothing?

Pet. And why not, pray?—But I did go there for nothing, though.—Do you think one must be paid for every thing?—If Mrs. Haller were to give me but a smiling look, I'd jump up to my neck in the great pond for nothing.

Fra. It seems then Mrs. Haller sent you?

Pet. Why, yes—But I'm not to talk about it.

Fra. Why so?

Pet. How should I know? "Look you," says Mrs. Haller, "Master Peter, be so good as not to mention it to any body." [*With much consequence.*] "Master Peter, be so good"—Hi! hi! hi!—"Master Peter, be so"—Hi! hi! hi!—

Fra. Oh! that is quite a different thing. Of course you must be silent then.

Pet. I know that; and so I am too. For I told old Tobias—says I, "Now, you're not to think as how Mrs. Haller sent the money; for I shall not say a word about that as long as I live," says I.

Fra. There you were very right. Did you carry him much money?

Pet. I don't know; I didn't count it. It was in a bit of a green purse. Mayhap it may be some little matter that she has scraped together in the last fortnight.

Fra. And why just in the last fortnight?

Pet. Because, about a fortnight since, I carried him some money before.

Fra. From Mrs. Haller?

Pet. Ay, sure; who else, think you? Father's not such a fool. He says it is our bounden duty, as christians, to take care of our money, and not give any thing away, especially in summer; for then, says he, there's herbs and roots enough in conscience to satisfy all the reasonable hungry poor. But I say father's wrong, and Mrs. Haller's right.

Fra. Yes, yes.—But this Mrs. Haller seems a strange woman, Peter.

Pet. Ay, at times she is plaguy odd. Why, she'll sit, and cry you a whole day through, without any one's knowing why.—Ay, and yet, somehow or other, whenever she cries, I always cry too—without knowing why.

Fra. [*To the* Stranger.] Are you satisfied?

Stra. Rid me of that babbler.

Fra. Good day, Master Peter.

Pet. You're not going yet, are you?

Fra. Mrs. Haller will be waiting for an answer.

Pet. So she will. And I have another place or two to call at. [*Takes off his hat to* Stranger.] Servant, sir!

Stra. Pshaw!—

Pet. Pshaw! What—he's angry. [Peter *turns to* Francis, *in a half whisper.*] He's angry, I suppose, because he can get nothing out of me.

Fra. It almost seems so.

Pet. Ay, I'd have him to know I'm no blab.

[*Exit.*

Fra. Now, sir?

Stra. What do you want?

Fra. Were you not wrong, sir?

Stra. Hem! wrong!

Fra. Can you still doubt?

Stra. I'll hear no more! Who is this Mrs. Haller? Why do I always follow her path? Go where I will, whenever I try to do good, she has always been before me.

Fra. You should rejoice at that.

Stra. Rejoice!

Fra. Surely! That there are other good and charitable people in the world beside yourself.

Stra. Oh, yes!

Fra. Why not seek to be acquainted with her? I saw her yesterday in the garden up at the Castle. Mr. Solomon, the steward, says she has been unwell, and confined to her room almost ever since we have been here. But one would not think it, to look at her; for a more beautiful creature I never saw.

Stra. So much the worse. Beauty is a mask.

Fra. In her it seems a mirror of the soul. Her charities—

Stra. Talk not to me of her charities. All women wish to be conspicuous:—in town by their wit; in the country by their heart.

Fra. 'Tis immaterial in what way good is done.

Stra. No; 'tis not immaterial.

Fra. To this poor old man at least.

Stra. He needs no assistance of mine.

Fra. His most urgent wants indeed, Mrs. Haller has relieved; but whether she has or could have given as much as would purchase liberty for the son, the prop of his age—

Stra. Silence! I will not give him a doit! [*In a peevish tone.*] You interest yourself very warmly in his behalf. Perhaps you are to be a sharer in the gift.

Fra. Sir, sir, that did not come from your heart.

Stra. [*Recollecting himself.*] Forgive me!

Fra. Poor master! How must the world have used you, before it could have instilled this hatred of mankind, this constant doubt of honesty and virtue!

Stra. Leave me to myself!

[*Throws himself on a seat; takes from his pocket "Zimmerman on Solitude," and reads.*

Fra. [*Aside, surveying him.*] Again reading! Thus it is from morn to night. To him nature has no beauty; life, no charm. For three years I have never seen him smile. What will be his fate at last? Nothing diverts him. Oh, if he would but attach himself to any living thing! Were it an animal—for something man must love.

Enter Tobias, *from the Hut.*

Tob. Oh! how refreshing, after seven long weeks, to feel these warm sun beams once again! Thanks! thanks! bounteous Heaven, for the joy I taste.

[*Presses his cap between his hands, looks up and prays.—The* Stranger *observes him attentively.*

Fra. [*To the* Stranger.] This old man's share of earthly happiness can be but little; yet mark how grateful he is for his portion of it.

Stra. Because, though old, he is but a child in the leading strings of Hope.

Fra. Hope is the nurse of life.

Stra. And her cradle is the grave.

[Tobias *replaces his cap.*

Fra. I wish you joy. I am glad to see you are so much recovered.

Tob. Thank you. Heaven, and the assistance of a kind lady, have saved me for another year or two.

Fra. How old are you, pray?

Tob. Seventy-six. To be sure I can expect but little joy before I die. Yet, there is another, and a better world.

Fra. To the unfortunate, then, death is scarce an evil?

Tob. Am I so unfortunate? Do I not enjoy this glorious morning? Am I not in health again! Believe me, sir, he, who, leaving the bed of sickness, for the first time breathes the fresh pure air, is, at that moment, the happiest of his Maker's creatures.

Fra. Yet 'tis a happiness that fails upon enjoyment.

Tob. True; but less so in old age. Some fifty years ago my father left me this cottage. I was a strong lad; and took an honest wife. Heaven blessed my farm with rich crops, and my marriage with five children. This lasted nine or ten years. Two of my children died. I felt it sorely. The land was afflicted with a famine. My wife assisted me in supporting our family: but four years after, she left our dwelling for a better place. And of my five children only one son remained. This was blow upon blow. It was long before I regained my fortitude. At length resignation and religion had their effect. I again attached myself to life. My son grew, and helped me in my work. Now the state has called him away to bear a musket. This is to me a loss indeed. I can work no more. I am old and weak; and true it is, but for Mrs. Haller, I must have perished.

Fra. Still then life has its charms for you?

Tob. Why not, while the world holds any thing that's dear to me? Have not I a son?

Fra. Who knows, that you will ever see him more? He may be dead.

Tob. Alas! he may. But as long as I am not sure of it, he lives to me: And if he falls, 'tis in his country's cause. Nay, should I lose him, still I should not wish to die. Here is the hut in which I was born. Here is the tree that grew with me; and, I am almost ashamed to confess it—I have a dog, I love.

Fra. A dog!

Tob. Yes!—Smile if you please: but hear me. My benefactress once came to my hut herself, some time before you fixed here. The poor animal, unused to see the form of elegance and beauty enter the door of penury, growled at her.—"I wonder you keep that surly, ugly animal, Mr. Tobias," said she; "you, who have hardly food enough for yourself."—"Ah, madam," I replied, "if I part with him, are you sure that any thing else will love me?"—She was pleased with my answer.

Fra. [*To* Stranger.] Excuse me, sir; but I wish you had listened.

Stra. I have listened.

Fra. Then, sir, I wish you would follow this poor old man's example.

Stra. [*Pauses.*] Here; take this book, and lay it on my desk. [*Francis goes into the Lodge with the book.*] How much has this Mrs. Haller given you?

Tob. Oh, sir, she has given me so much, that I can look towards winter without fear.

Stra. No more?

Tob. What could I do with more?—Ah! true; I might—

Stra. I know it.—You might buy your son's release.—There! [*Presses a purse into his hand, and exit.*

Tob. What is all this? [*Opens the purse, and finds it full of gold.*] Merciful Heaven!—

Enter Francis.

—Now look, sir: is confidence in Heaven unrewarded?

Fra. I wish you joy! My master gave you this!

Tob. Yes, your noble master. Heaven reward him!

Fra. Just like him. He sent me with his book, that no one might be witness to his bounty.

Tob. He would not even take my thanks. He was gone before I could speak.

Fra. Just his way.

Tob. Now, I'll go as quick as these old legs will bear me. What a delightful errand! I go to release my Robert! How the lad will rejoice! There is a girl too, in the village, that will rejoice with him. O Providence, how good art thou! Years of distress never can efface the recollection of former happiness; but one joyful moment drives from the memory an age of misery.

[*Exit.*

Fra. [*Looks after him.*] Why am I not wealthy? 'Sdeath! why am I not a prince! I never thought myself envious; but I feel I am. Yes, I must envy those who, with the will, have the power to do good.

[*Exit.*

SCENE II.

An Antichamber in Wintersen Castle.

Enter Susan, *meeting Footmen with table and chairs.*

Susan. Why, George! Harry! where have you been loitering? Put down these things. Mrs. Haller has been calling for you this half hour.

Geo. Well, here I am then. What does she want with me?

Susan. That she will tell you herself. Here she comes.

Enter Mrs. Haller, *(with a letter, a* Maid *following.*

Mrs. H. Very well; if those things are done, let the drawing room be made ready immediately.—[*Exit* Maids.] And, George, run immediately into the park, and tell Mr. Solomon I wish to speak with him. [*Exit* Footman.] I cannot understand this. I do not learn whether their coming to this place be but the whim of a moment, or a plan for a longer stay: if the latter, farewell, solitude! farewell, study!—farewell!—Yes, I must make room for gaiety, and mere frivolity. Yet could I willingly submit to all; but, should the Countess give me new proofs of her attachment, perhaps of her respect, Oh! how will my conscience upbraid me! Or—I shudder at the thought! if this seat be visited by company, and chance should conduct hither any of my former acquaintance—Alas! alas! how wretched is the being who fears the sight of any one fellow-creature! But, oh! superior misery! to dread still more the presence of a former friend!—Who's there?

Enter Peter.

Pet. Nobody. It's only me.

Mrs. H. So soon returned?

Pet. Sharp lad, a'n't I? On the road I've had a bit of talk too, and—

Mrs. H. But you have observed my directions!

Pet. Oh, yes, yes:—I told old Tobias as how he would never know as long as he lived that the money came from you.

Mrs. H. You found him quite recovered, I hope?

Pet. Ay, sure did I. He's coming out to-day for the first time.

Mrs. H. I rejoice to hear it.

Pet. He said that he was obliged to you for all; and before dinner would crawl up to thank you.

Mrs. H. Good Peter, do me another service.

Pet. Ay, a hundred, if you'll only let me have a good long stare at you.

Mrs. H. With all my heart! Observe when old Tobias comes, and send him away. Tell him I am busy, or asleep, or unwell, or what you please.

Pet. I will, I will.

Sol. [*Without.*] There, there, go to the post-office.

Mrs. H. Oh! here comes Mr. Solomon.

Pet. What! Father?—Ay, so there is. Father's a main clever man: he knows what's going on all over the world.

Mrs. H. No wonder; for you know he receives as many letters as a prime minister and all his secretaries.

Enter Solomon.

Sol. Good morning, good morning to you, Mrs. Haller. It gives me infinite pleasure to see you look so charmingly well. You have had the goodness to send for your humble servant. Any news from the Great City? There are very weighty matters in agitation. I have my letters too.

Mrs. H. [*Smiling.*] I think, Mr. Solomon, you must correspond with the four quarters of the globe.

Sol. Beg pardon, not with the whole world, Mrs. Haller: but [*Consequentially.*] to be sure I have correspondents, on whom I can rely, in the chief cities of Europe, Asia, Africa, and America.

Mrs. H. And yet I have my doubts whether you know what is to happen this very day at this very place.

Sol. At this very place! Nothing material. We meant to have sown a little barley to-day, but the ground is too dry; and the sheep-shearing is not to be till to-morrow.

Pet. No, nor the bull-baiting till—

Sol. Hold your tongue, blockhead! Get about your business.

Pet. Blockhead! There again! I suppose I'm not to open my mouth. [*To* Mrs. Haller.] Good bye!

[*Exit.*

Mrs. H. The Count will be here to-day.

Sol. How! What!

Mrs. H. With his lady, and his brother-in-law, Baron Steinfort.

Sol. My letters say nothing of this. You are laughing at your humble servant.

Mrs. H. You know, sir, I'm not much given to jesting.

Sol. Peter!—Good lack-a-day!—His Right Honourable Excellency Count Wintersen, and her Right Honourable Excellency the Countess Wintersen, and his Honourable Lordship Baron Steinfort—And, Lord have mercy! nothing in proper order!—Here, Peter! Peter!

Enter Peter.

Pet. Well, now; what's the matter again?

Sol. Call all the house together directly! Send to the game keeper; tell him to bring some venison. Tell Rebecca to uncase the furniture, and take the covering from the Venetian looking glasses, that her Right Honourable Ladyship the Countess may look at her gracious countenance: and tell the cook to let me see him without loss of time: and tell John to catch a brace or two of carp. And tell—and tell—and tell—tell Frederick to friz my Sunday wig.— Mercy on us!—Tell—There—Go!— [*Exit* Peter.] Heavens and earth! so little of the new furnishing of this old castle is completed!—Where are we to put his Honourable Lordship the Baron?

Mrs. H. Let him have the little chamber at the head of the stairs; it is a neat room, and commands a beautiful prospect.

Sol. Very right, very right. But that room has always been occupied by the Count's private secretary. Suppose!—Hold, I have it. You know the little lodge at the end of the park: we can thrust the secretary into that.

Mrs. H. You forget, Mr. Solomon; you told me that the Stranger lived there.

Sol. Pshaw! What have we to do with the Stranger?—Who told him to live there?—He must turn out.

Mrs. H. That would be unjust; for you said, that you let the dwelling to him, and by your own account he pays well for it.

Sol. He does, he does. But nobody knows who he is. The devil himself can't make him out. To be sure, I lately received a letter from Spain, which informed me that a spy had taken up his abode in this country, and from the description—

Mrs. H. A spy! Ridiculous! Every thing I have heard bespeaks him to be a man, who may be allowed to dwell any where. His life is solitude and silence.

Sol. So it is.

Mrs. H. You tell me too he does much good.

Sol. That he does.

Mrs. H. He hurts nothing; not the worm in his way.

Sol. That he does not.

Mrs. H. He troubles no one.

Sol. True! true!

Mrs. H. Well, what do you want more?

Sol. I want to know who he is. If the man would only converse a little, one might have an opportunity of *pumping*; but if one meets him in the lime walk, or by the river, it is nothing but—"Good morrow;"—and off he marches. Once or twice I have contrived to edge in a word—"Fine day."—"Yes."—"Taking a little exercise, I perceive."—"Yes:"—and off again like a shot. The devil take such close fellows, say I. And, like master like man; not a syllable do I know of that mumps his servant, except that his name is Francis.

Mrs. H. You are putting yourself into a passion, and quite forget who are expected.

Sol. So I do—Mercy on us!—There now, you see what misfortunes arise from not knowing people.

Mrs. H. 'Tis near twelve o'clock already! If his lordship has stolen an hour from his usual sleep, the family must soon be here. I go to my duty; you will attend to yours, Mr. Solomon.

[*Exit.*

Sol. Yes, I'll look after my duty, never fear. There goes another of the same class. Nobody knows who she is again. However, thus much I do know of her, that her Right Honourable Ladyship the Countess, all at once, popped her into the house, like a blot of ink upon a sheet of paper. But why, wherefore, or for what reason, not a soul can tell.—"She is to manage the family within doors." She to manage! Fire and faggots! Haven't I managed every thing within and without, most reputably, these twenty years? I must own I grow a little old, and she does take a deal of pains: but all this she learned of me. When she first came here—Mercy on us! she didn't know that linen was made of flax. But what was to be expected from one who has no foreign correspondence.

[*Exit.*

ACT THE SECOND.

SCENE I.

A Drawing Room in the Castle, with a Piano Forte, Harp, Music, Bookstand, Sofas, Chairs, Tables, &c.

Enter Solomon.

Sol. Well, for once I think I have the advantage of Madam Haller. Such a dance have I provided to welcome their Excellencies, and she quite out of the the secret! And such a hornpipe by the little Brunette! I'll have a rehearsal first though, and then surprise their honours after dinner.

[*Flourish of rural music without.*

Pet. [*Without.*] Stop; not yet, not yet: but make way there, make way, my good friends, tenants, and villagers.—John! George! Frederick! Good friends, make way.

Sol. It is not the Count: it's only Baron Steinfort. Stand back, I say; and stop the music!

Enter Baron Steinfort, *ushered in by* Peter *and* Footmen. Peter *mimicks and apes his father.*

Sol. I have the honour to introduce to your lordship myself, Mr. Solomon, who blesses the hour in which fortune allows him to become acquainted with the Honourable Baron Steinfort, brother-in-law of his Right Honourable Excellency Count Wintersen, my noble master.

Pet. Bless our noble master!

Bar. Old and young, I see they'll allow me no peace. [*Aside.*] Enough, enough, good Mr. Solomon. I am a soldier. I pay but few compliments, and require as few from others.

Sol. I beg, my lord—We do live in the country to be sure, but we are acquainted with the reverence due to exalted personages.

Pet. Yes—We are acquainted with exalted personages.

Bar. What is to become of me?—Well, well, I hope we shall be better acquainted. You must know, Mr. Solomon, I intend to assist, for a couple of months at least, in attacking the well stocked cellars of Wintersen.

Sol. Why not whole years, my lord?—Inexpressible would be the satisfaction of your humble servant. And, though I say it, well stocked indeed are our cellars. I have, in every respect, here managed matters in so frugal and provident a way, that his Right Honourable Excellency the Count, will be astonished. [Baron *yawns.*] Extremely sorry it is not in my power to entertain your lordship.

Pet. Extremely sorry.

Sol. Where can Mrs. Haller have hid herself?

Bar. Mrs. Haller! who is she?

Sol. Why, who she is, I can't exactly tell your lordship.

Pet. No, nor I.

Sol. None of my correspondents give any account of her. She is here in the capacity of a kind of a superior housekeeper. Methinks, I hear her silver voice upon the stairs. I will have the honour of sending her to your lordship in an instant.

Bar. Oh! don't trouble yourself.

Sol. No trouble whatever! I remain, at all times, your honourable lordship's most obedient, humble, and devoted servant.

[*Exit, bowing.*

Pet. Devoted servant.

[*Exit, bowing.*

Bar. Now for a fresh plague. Now am I to be tormented by some chattering old ugly hag, till I am stunned with her noise and officious hospitality. Oh, patience! what a virtue art thou!

Enter Mrs. Haller, *with a becoming curtsey.* Baron *rises, and returns a bow, in confusion.*

[*Aside.*] No, old she is not. [*Casts another glance at her.*] No, by Jove, nor ugly.

Mrs. H. I rejoice, my lord, in thus becoming acquainted with the brother of my benefactress.

Bar. Madam, that title shall be doubly valuable to me, since it gives me an introduction equally to be rejoiced at.

Mrs. H. [*Without attending to the compliment.*] This lovely weather, then, has enticed the Count from the city?

Bar. Not exactly that. You know him. Sunshine or clouds are to him alike, as long as eternal summer reigns in his own heart and family.

Mrs. H. The Count possesses a most cheerful and amiable philosophy. Ever in the same happy humour; ever enjoying each minute of his life. But you must confess, my lord, that he is a favourite child of fortune, and has much to be grateful to her for. Not merely because she has given him birth and riches, but for a native sweetness of temper, never to be acquired; and a graceful suavity of manners, whose school must be the mind. And, need I enumerate among fortune's favours, the hand and affections of your accomplished sister?

Bar. [*More and more struck as her understanding opens upon him.*] True, madam. My good easy brother, too, seems fully sensible of his happiness, and is resolved to retain it. He has quitted the service to live here. I am yet afraid he may soon grow weary of Wintersen and retirement.

Mrs. H. I should trust not. They, who bear a cheerful and unreproaching conscience into solitude, surely must increase the measure of their own enjoyments. They quit the poor, precarious, the dependent pleasures, which they borrowed from the world, to draw a real bliss from that exhaustless source of true delight, the fountain of a pure unsullied heart.

Bar. Has retirement long possessed so lovely an advocate?

Mrs. H. I have lived here three years.

Bar. And never felt a secret wish for the society you left, and must have adorned?

Mrs. H. Never.

Bar. To feel thus belongs either to a very rough or a very polished soul. The first sight convinced me in which class I am to place you.

Mrs. H. [*With a sigh.*] There may, perhaps, be a third class.

Bar. Indeed, madam, I wish not to be thought forward; but women always seemed to me less calculated for retirement than men. We have a thousand employments, a thousand amusements, which you have not.

Mrs. H. Dare I ask what they are?

Bar. We ride—we hunt—we play—read—write.—

Mrs. H. The noble employments of the chase, and the still more noble employment of play, I grant you.

Bar. Nay, but dare I ask what are your employments for a day?

Mrs. H. Oh, my lord! you cannot imagine how quickly time passes when a certain uniformity guides the minutes of our life. How often do I ask, "Is Saturday come again so soon?" On a bright cheerful morning, my books and breakfast are carried out upon the grass plot. Then is the sweet picture of reviving industry and eager innocence always new to me. The birds' notes so often heard, still waken new ideas: the herds are led into the fields: the peasant bends his eye upon his plough. Every thing lives and moves; and in every creature's mind it seems as it were morning. Towards evening I begin to roam abroad: from the park into the meadows. And sometimes, returning, I pause to look at the village boys and girls as they play. Then do I bless their innocence, and pray to Heaven, those laughing, thoughtless hours, could be their lot for ever.

Bar. This is excellent!—But these are summer amusements.—The winter! the winter!

Mrs. H. Why for ever picture winter like old age, torpid, tedious, and uncheerful? Winter has its own delights: this is the time to instruct and mend the mind by reading and reflection. At this season, too, I often take my harp, and amuse myself by playing or singing the little favourite airs that remind me of the past, or solicit hope for the future.

Bar. Happy indeed are they who can thus create, and vary their own pleasures and employments.

Enter Peter.

Pet. Well—well—Pray now—I was ordered—I can keep him back no longer—He will come in.

Enter Tobias, *forcing his way.*

Tob. I must, good Heaven, I must!

Mrs. H. [*Confused.*] I have no time at present—I—I—You see I am not alone.

Tob. Oh! this good gentleman will forgive me.

Bar. What do you want?

Tob. To return thanks. Even charity is a burden if one may not be grateful for it.

Mrs. H. To-morrow, good Tobias; to-morrow.

Bar. Nay, no false delicacy, madam. Allow him to vent the feelings of his heart; and permit me to witness a scene which convinces me, even more powerfully than your conversation, how nobly you employ your time. Speak, old man.

Tob. Oh, lady, that each word which drops from my lips, might call down a blessing on your head! I lay forsaken and dying in my hut: not even bread nor hope remained. Oh! then you came in the form of an angel, brought medicines to me; and your sweet consoling voice did more than those. I am recovered. To-day, for the first time, I have returned thanks in presence of the sun: and now I come to you, noble lady. Let me drop my tears upon your charitable hand. For your sake, Heaven has blessed my latter days. The Stranger too, who lives near me, has given me a purse of gold to buy my son's release. I am on my way to the city: I shall purchase my Robert's release. Then I shall have an honest daughter-in-law. And you, if ever after that you pass our happy cottage, oh! what must you feel when you say to yourself, "This is my work!"

Mrs. H. [*In a tone of entreaty.*] Enough, Tobias; enough!

Tob. I beg pardon! I cannot utter what is breathing in my breast. There is One, who knows it. May His blessing and your own heart reward you.

[*Exit,* Peter *following.* Mrs. Haller *casts her eyes upon the ground, and contends against the confusion of an exalted soul, when surprised in a good action. The* Baron *stands opposite to her, and from time to time casts a glance at her, in which his heart is swimming.*

Mrs. H. [*Endeavouring to bring about a conversation.*] I suppose, my lord, we may expect the Count and Countess every moment now?

Bar. Not just yet, madam. He travels at his leisure. I am selfish, perhaps, in not being anxious for his speed: the delay has procured me a delight which I never shall forget.

Mrs. H. [*Smiling.*] You satirise mankind, my lord.

Bar. How so?

Mrs. H. In supposing such scenes to be uncommon.

Bar. I confess I was little prepared for such an acquaintance as yourself: I am extremely surprised. When Solomon told me your name and situation, how could I suppose that—Pardon my curiosity: You have been, or are married?

Mrs. H. [*Suddenly sinking from her cheerful raillery into mournful gloom.*] I have been married, my lord.

Bar. [*Whose enquiries evince his curiosity, yet are restrained within the bounds of the nicest respect.*] A widow, then?

Mrs. H. I beseech you—There are strings in the human heart, which touched, will sometimes utter dreadful discord—I beseech you—

Bar. I understand you. I see you know how to conceal every thing except your perfections.

Mrs. H. My perfections, alas!—[*Rural music without.*] But I hear the happy tenantry announce the Count's arrival. Your pardon, my lord; I must attend them.

[*Exit.*

Bar. Excellent creature!—What is she, and what can be her history? I must seek my sister instantly. How strong and how sudden is the interest I feel for her! But it is a feeling I ought to check. And yet, why so? Whatever are the emotions she has inspired, I am sure they arise from the perfections of her mind: and never shall they be met with unworthiness in mine.

[*Exit.*

SCENE II.

The Lawn.

Solomon *and* Peter *are discovered arranging the* Tenantry.—*Rural music.*

Enter Count *and* Countess Wintersen, *(the latter leading her Child,) the* Baron, Mrs. Haller, Charlotte, *and* Servants *following.*

Sol. Welcome, ten thousand welcomes, your Excellencies. Some little preparation made for welcome too. But that will be seen anon.

Count. Well! here we are! Heaven bless our advance and retreat! Mrs. Haller, I bring you an invalid, who in future will swear to no flag but yours.

Mrs. H. Mine flies for retreat and rural happiness.

Count. But not without retreating graces, and retiring cupids too.

Countess. [*Who has in the mean time kindly embraced* Mrs. Haller, *and by her been welcomed to Wintersen.*] My dear Count, you forget that I am present.

Count. Why, in the name of chivalry, how can I do less than your gallant brother, the Baron? who has been so kind as nearly to kill my four greys, in order to be here five minutes before me.

Bar. Had I known all the charms of this place, you should have said so with justice.

Countess. Don't you think William much grown?

Mrs. H. The sweet boy!

[*Stoops to kiss him, and deep melancholy overshadows her countenance.*

Count. Well, Solomon, you've provided a good dinner?

Sol. As good as haste would allow, please your Right Honourable Excellency!

Pet. Yes, as good as—

[Count *goes aside with* Solomon *and* Peter.

Bar. Tell me, I conjure you, sister, what jewel you have thus buried in the country?

Countess. Ha! ha! ha! What, brother, you caught at last?

Bar. Answer me.

Countess. Well, her name is Mrs. Haller.

Bar. That I know; but—

Countess. But!—but I know no more myself.

Bar. Jesting apart, I wish to know.

Countess. And, jesting apart, I wish you would not plague me. I have at least a hundred thousand important things to do. Heavens! the vicar may come to pay his respects to me before I have been at my toilet; of course I must consult my looking-glass on the occasion. Come, William, will you help to dress me, or stay with your father?

Count. We'll take care of him.

Countess. Come, Mrs. Haller.

[*Exit with* Mrs. Haller, Charlotte *following.*

Bar. [*Aside, and going.*] I am in a very singular humour.

Count. Whither so fast, good brother?

Bar. To my apartment: I have letters to—I—

Count. Pshaw! stay. Let us take a turn in the park together.

Bar. Excuse me. I am not perfectly well. I should be but bad company. I—

[*Exit.—The* Tenantry *retire.*

Count. Well, Solomon, you are as great a fool as ever, I see.

Sol. Ha! ha! At your Right Honourable Excellency's service.

Count. [*Points to* Peter.] Who is that ape in the corner?

Sol. Ape!—Oh! that is—with respect to your Excellency be it spoken—the son of my body; by name, Peter.

[Peter *bows.*

Count. So, so! Well, how goes all on?

Sol. Well and good; well and good. Your Excellency will see how I've improved the park: You'll not know it again. A hermitage here; serpentine walks there; an obelisk; a ruin; and all so sparingly, all done with the most economical economy.

Count. Well, I'll have a peep at your obelisk and ruins, while they prepare for dinner!

Sol. I have already ordered it, and will have the honour of attending your Right Honourable Excellency.

Count. Come, lead the way. Peter, attend your young master to the house; we must not tire him.

[*Exit, conducted by* Solomon.

Pet. We'll go round this way, your little Excellency, and then we shall see the bridge as we go by; and the new boat, with all the fine ribbands and streamers. This way, your little Excellency.

[*Exit, leading the Child.*

SCENE III.

The Antichamber.

Enter Mrs. Haller.

Mrs. H. What has thus alarmed and subdued me? My tears flow; my heart bleeds. Already had I apparently overcome my chagrin: already had I at least assumed that easy gaiety once so natural to me, when the sight of this child in an instant overpowered me. When the Countess called him William—Oh! she knew not that she plunged a poniard in my heart. I have a William too, who must be as tall as this, if he be still alive. Ah! yes, if he be still alive. His little sister too! Why, fancy, dost thou rack me thus? Why dost thou image my poor children, fainting in sickness, and crying to their mother? To the mother who has abandoned them? [*Weeps.*] What a wretched outcast am I! And that just to-day I should be doomed to feel these horrible emotions! just to-day, when disguise was so necessary.

Enter Charlotte.

Char. [*Entering.*] Very pretty, very pretty indeed; better send me to the garret at once. Your servant, Mrs. Haller. I beg, madam, I may have a room fit for a respectable person.

Mrs. H. The chamber into which you have been shown is, I think, a very neat one.

Char. A very neat one, is it? Up the back stairs, and over the laundry! I should never be able to close my eyes.

Mrs. H. [*Very mildly.*] I slept there a whole year.

Char. Did you? Then I advise you to remove into it again, and the sooner the better. I'd have you to know, madam, there is a material difference between certain persons and certain persons. Much depends upon the manner in which one has been educated. I think, madam, it would only be proper if you resigned your room to me.

Mrs. H. If the Countess desires it, certainly.

Char. The Countess! Very pretty, indeed! Would you have me think of plaguing her ladyship with such trifles? I shall order my trunk to be carried where-ever I please.

Mrs. H. Certainly; only not into my chamber.

Char. Provoking creature! But how could I expect to find breeding among creatures born of one knows not whom, and coming one knows not whence?

Mrs. H. The remark is very just.

Enter Peter, *in haste.*

Pet. Oh lud! Oh lud! Oh lud! Oh lud!

Mrs. H. What's the matter?

Pet. The child has fallen into the river! His little Excellency is drowned!

Mrs. H. Who? What?

Pet. His honour, my young master!

Mrs. H. Drowned?

Pet. Yes.

Mrs. H. Dead?

Pet. No; he's not dead.

Mrs. H. Well, well, then softly;—you will alarm the Countess.

Enter the Baron.

Bar. What is the matter? Why all this noise?

Pet. Noise? why—

Mrs. H. Be not alarmed, my lord. Whatever may have happened, the dear child is now at least safe. You said so, I think, master Peter?

Pet. Why, to be sure, his little Excellency is not hurt; but he's very wet though: and the Count is taking him by the garden door to the house.

Bar. Right, that the countess may not be alarmed. But tell us, young man, how could it happen?

Pet. From beginning to end?

Mrs. H. Never mind particulars. You attended the dear child?

Pet. True.

Mrs. H. Into the park?

Pet. True.

Mrs. H. And then you went to the river?

Pet. True.—Why, rabbit it, I believe you're a witch.

Mrs. H. Well, and what happened further?

Pet. Why, you see, his dear little Excellency would see the bridge, that father built out of the old summer house; and the streamers, and the boat, and all that.—I only turned my head round for a moment, to look after a magpie—crush! down went the bridge, with his little Excellency; and oh, how I was scared to see him carried down the river!

Bar. And you drew him out again directly?

Pet. No, I didn't.

Mrs. H. No; your father did?

Pet. No, he didn't.

Mrs. H. Why you did not leave him in the water?

Pet. Yes, we did!—But we bawled as loud as we could; you might have heard us down to the village.

Mrs. H. Ay—and so the people came immediately to his assistance.

Pet. No, they didn't: but the Stranger came, that lives yonder, close to old Toby, and never speaks a syllable. Odsbodlikins! what a devil of a fellow it is! With a single spring bounces he slap into the torrent; sails and dives about and about like a duck; gets me hold of the little angel's hair, and, Heaven bless him! pulls him safe and sound to dry land again.—Ha! ha! ha!

Bar. Is the Stranger with them?

Pet. Oh lud! no. He ran away. His Excellency wanted to thank him, and all that; but he was off; vanquished like a ghost.

Enter Solomon.

Sol. Oh! thou careless varlet! I disown you! What an accident might have happened! and how you have terrified his Excellency! But I beg pardon, [*Bows.*] His Right Honourable Excellency, the Count, requests your—

Bar. We come.

[*Exit, with* Mrs. Haller.

Char. Ha! ha! ha! Why, Mr. Solomon, you seem to have a hopeful pupil.

Sol. Ah! sirrah!

Char. But, Mr. Solomon, why were you not nimble enough to have saved his young lordship?

Sol. Not in time, my sweet Miss. Besides, mercy on us! I should have sunk like a lump of lead: and I happened to have a letter of consequence in my pocket, which would have been made totally illegible; a letter from Constantinople, written by Chevalier— What's his name? [*Draws a letter from his pocket, and putting it up again directly, drops it.* Peter *takes it up, slily and unobserved.*] It contains momentous matter, I assure you. The world will be astonished when it comes to light; and not a soul will suppose that old Solomon had a finger in the pye.

Char. No, that I believe.

Sol. But I must go and see to the cellar. Miss, your most obedient servant.

[*Exit.*

Char. [*With pride.*] Your servant, Mr. Solomon.

Pet. Here's the letter from Constantinople. I wonder what it can be about. Now for it!

[*Opens it.*

Char. Aye, let us have it.

Pet. [Reads.] *If so be you say so, I'll never work for you, never no more. Considering as how your Sunday waistcoat has been turned three times, it doesn't look amiss, and I've charged as little as any tailor of 'em all. You say I must pay for the buckram; but I say, I'll be damn'd if I do. So no more from your loving nephew,*

Timothy Twist.

From Constantinople! Why, cousin Tim writ it.

Char. Cousin Tim! Who is he?

Pet. Good lack! Don't you know cousin Tim? Why, he's one of the best tailors in all—

Char. A tailor! No, sir, I do not know him. My father was state coachman, and wore his highness's livery.

[*Exit.*

Pet. [*Mimicking.*] "My father was state coachman, and wore his Highness's livery"—Well, and cousin Tim could have made his Highness's livery, if you go to that. State coachman, indeed!

[*Going.*

Enter Solomon.

Sol. Peter, you ninny, stay where you are. Is that chattering girl gone? Didn't I tell you we would have a practice of our dance? they are all ready on the lawn. Mark me; I represent the Count, and you the Baron.

[*Exit, with affected dignity.* Peter *follows, mimicking.*

SCENE IV.

The Lawn.—Seats placed.—Rustic Music.—Dancers are discovered as ready to perform.

Solomon *and* Peter *enter, and seat themselves.*

A Dance, in which the Dancers pay their reverence to Solomon *and* Peter *as they pass. At the end,* Solomon *and* Peter *strut off before the Dancers.*

ACT THE THIRD.

SCENE I.

The Skirts of the Park and Lodge, &c. as before. The Stranger *is discovered on a seat, reading.*

Enter Francis.

Fra. Sir, sir, dinner is ready.

Stra. I want no dinner.

Fra. I've got something good.

Stra. Eat it yourself.

Fra. You are not hungry?

Stra. No.

[*Rises.*

Fra. Nor I. The heat takes away all appetite.

Stra. Yes.

Fra. I'll put it by; perhaps at night—

Stra. Perhaps.

Fra. Dear sir, dare I speak?

Stra. Speak.

Fra. You have done a noble action.

Stra. What?

Fra. You have saved a fellow creature's life.

Stra. Peace.

Fra. Do you know who he was?

Stra. No.

Fra. The only son of Count Wintersen.

Stra. Immaterial.

Fra. A gentleman, by report, worthy and benevolent as yourself.

Stra. [*Angry.*] Silence! Dare you flatter me?

Fra. As I look to Heaven for mercy, I speak from my heart. When I observe how you are doing good around you, how you are making every individual's wants your own, and are yet yourself unhappy, alas! my heart bleeds for you.

Stra. I thank you, Francis. I can only thank you. Yet share this consolation with me:—my sufferings are unmerited.

Fra. My poor master!

Stra. Have you forgotten what the old man said this morning? "There is another and a better world!" Oh, 'twas true. Then let us hope with fervency, and yet endure with patience!—What's here?

Enter Charlotte, *from the Park gate.*

Char. I presume, sir, you are the strange gentleman that drew my young master out of the water?—[*The* Stranger *reads.*] Or [*To* Francis.] are you he? [Francis *makes a wry face.*] Are the creatures both dumb? [*Looks at them by turns.*] Surely, old Solomon has fixed two statues here, by way of ornament; for of any use there is no sign. [*Approaches* Francis.] No, this is alive, and breathes; yes, and moves its eyes. [*Bawls in his ear.*] Good friend!

Fra. I'm not deaf.

Char. No, nor dumb, I perceive at last.—Is yon lifeless thing your master?

Fra. That honest silent gentleman is my master.

Char. The same that drew the young Count out of the water?

Fra. The same.

Char. [*To the* Stranger.] Sir, my master and mistress, the Count and Countess, present their respectful compliments, and request the honour of your company at a family supper this evening.

Stra. I shall not come.

Char. But you'll scarce send such an uncivil answer as this. The Count is overpowered with gratitude. You saved his son's life.

Stra. I did it willingly.

Char. And won't accept of, "I thank you," in return?

Stra. No.

Char. You really are cruel, sir, I must tell you. There are three of us ladies at the Castle, and we are all dying with curiosity to know who you are. [*Exit* Stranger.] The master is crabbed enough, however. Let me try what I can make of the man. Pray, sir— [Francis *turns his back to her.*] —The beginning promises little enough. Friend, why won't you look at me.

Fra. I like to look at green trees better than green eyes.

Char. Green eyes, you monster! Who told you, that my eyes were green? Let me tell you there have been sonnets made on my eyes, before now.

Fra. Glad to hear it.

Char. To the point then at once. What is your master?

Fra. A man.

Char. I surmised as much. But what's his name?

Fra. The same as his father's.

Char. Not unlikely;—and his father was—

Fra. Married.

Char. To whom?

Fra. To a woman.

Char. [*Enraged.*] I'll tell you what; who your master is I see I shall not learn, and I don't care; but I know what you are.

Fra. Well, what am I?

Char. A bear!

[*Exit.*

Fra. Thank you! Now to see how habit and example corrupt one's manners. I am naturally the civilest spoken fellow in the world to the pretty prattling rogues; yet, following my master's humour, I've rudely driven this wench away. I must have a peep at her though.

[*Looking towards the Park gate.*

Enter Stranger.

Stra. Is that woman gone?

Fra. Yes.

Stra. Francis!

Fra. Sir.

Stra. We must be gone too.

Fra. But whither?

Stra. I don't care.

Fra. I'll attend you.

Stra. To any place?

Fra. To death.

Stra. Heav'n grant it—to me, at least! There is peace.

Fra. Peace is every where. Let the storm rage without, if the heart be but at rest. Yet I think we are very well where we are: the situation is inviting; and nature lavish of her beauties, and of her bounties too.

Stra. But I am not a wild beast, to be stared at, and sent for as a show. Is it fit I should be?

Fra. Another of your interpretations! That a man, the life of whose only son you have saved, should invite you to his house, seems to me not very unnatural.

Stra. I will not be invited to any house.

Fra. For once, methinks, you might submit. You'll not be asked a second time.

Stra. Proud wretches! They believe the most essential service is requited, if one may but have the honour of sitting at their table. Let us begone.

Fra. Yet hold, sir! This bustle will soon be over. Used to the town, the Count and his party will soon be tired of simple nature, and you will again be freed from observation.

Stra. Not from your's.

Fra. This is too much. Do I deserve your doubts?

Stra. Am I in the wrong?

Fra. You are indeed!

Stra. Francis, my servant, you are my only friend.

Fra. That title makes amends for all.

Stra. But look, Francis; there are uniforms and gay dresses in the walk again. No, I must be gone. Here I'll stay no longer.

Fra. Well then, I'll tie up my bundle.

Stra. The sooner the better! They come this way. Now must I shut myself in my hovel, and lose this fine breeze. Nay, if they be your highbred class of all, they may have impudence enough to walk into my chamber. Francis, I shall lock the door.

[*Goes into the Lodge, locks the door, and fastens the shutters.*

Fra. And I'll be your centinel.

Stra. Very well.

Fra. Now should these people be as inquisitive as their maid, I must summon my whole stock of impertinence. But their questions and my answers need little study. They can learn nothing of the Stranger from me; for the best of all possible reasons—I know nothing myself.

Enter Baron *and* Countess.

Countess. There is a strange face. The servant probably.

Bar. Friend, can we speak to your master?

Fra. No.

Bar. Only for a few minutes.

Fra. He has locked himself in his room.

Countess. Tell him a lady waits for him.

Fra. Then he's sure not to come.

Countess. Does he hate our sex?

Fra. He hates the whole human race, but woman particularly.

Countess. And why?

Fra. He may perhaps have been deceived.

Countess. This is not very courteous.

Fra. My master is not over courteous: but when he sees a chance of saving a fellow creature's life, he'll attempt it at the hazard of his own.

Bar. You are right. Now hear the reason of our visit. The wife and brother-in-law of the man, whose child your master has saved, wish to acknowledge their obligations to him.

Fra. That he dislikes. He only wishes to live unnoticed.

Countess. He appears to be unfortunate.

Fra. Appears!

Countess. An affair of honour, perhaps, or some unhappy attachment may have—

Fra. They may.

Countess. Be this as it may, I wish to know who he is.

Fra. So do I.

Countess. What! don't you know him yourself?

Fra. Oh! I know him well enough. I mean his real self—His heart—his soul—his worth—his honour!—Perhaps you think one knows a man, when one is acquainted with his name and person.

Countess. 'Tis well said, friend; you please me much. And now I should like to know you. Who are you?

Fra. Your humble servant.

[*Exit.*

Countess. This is affectation! A desire to appear singular! Every one wishes to make himself distinguished. One sails round the world; another creeps into a hovel.

Bar. And the man apes his master!

Countess. Come, brother, let us seek the Count. He and Mrs. Haller turned into the lawn—

[*Going.*

Bar. Stay. First a word or two, sister. I am in love.

Countess. For the hundreth time.

Bar. For the first time in my life.

Countess. I wish you joy.

Bar. Till now you have evaded my inquiries. Who is she? I beseech you, sister, be serious. There is a time for all things.

Countess. Bless us! Why you look as if you were going to raise a spirit. Don't fix your eyes so earnestly. Well, if I am to be serious, I obey. I do not know who Mrs. Haller is, as I have already told you; but what I do know of her, shall not be concealed from you. It may now be three years ago, when, one evening, about twilight, a lady was announced, who wished to speak to me in private. Mrs. Haller appeared with all that grace and modesty, which have enchanted you. Her features, at that moment, bore keener marks of the sorrow and confusion which have since settled into gentle melancholy. She threw herself at my feet; and besought me to save a wretch who was on the brink of despair. She told me she had heard much of my benevolence, and offered herself as a servant to attend me. I endeavoured to dive into the cause of her sufferings, but in vain. She concealed her secret; yet opened to me more and more each day a heart, chosen by virtue as her temple, and an understanding improved by the most refined attainments. She no longer remained my servant, but became my friend; and, by her own desire, has ever since resided here. [*Curtseying.*] Brother, I have done.

Bar. Too little to satisfy my curiosity; yet enough to make me realise my project. Sister, lend me your aid—I would marry her.

Countess. You!

Bar. I.

Countess. Baron Steinfort.

Bar. For shame! If I understand you!

Countess. Not so harsh, and not so hasty! Those great sentiments of contempt of inequality in rank are very fine in a romance; but we happen not to be inhabitants of an ideal world. How could you introduce her to the circle we live in? You surely would not attempt to present her to—

Bar. Object as you will—my answer is—*I love.* Sister, you see a man before you, who—

Countess. Who wants a wife.

Bar. No; who has deliberately poised advantage against disadvantage; domestic ease and comfort against the false gaieties of fashion. I can withdraw into the country. I need no honours to make my tenants happy; and my heart will teach me to make their happiness my own. With such a wife as this, children who resemble her, and fortune enough to spread comfort around me, what would the soul of man have more?

Countess. This is all vastly fine. I admire your plan; only you seem to have forgotten one trifling circumstance.

Bar. And that is—

Countess. Whether Mrs. Haller will have you or not.

Bar. There, sister, I just want your assistance.—[*Seizing her hand.*] Good Henrietta!

Countess. Well, here's my hand. I'll do all I can for you. St!—We had near been overheard. They are coming. Be patient and obedient.

Enter Count, *and* Mrs. Haller, *leaning on his arm.*

Count. Upon my word, Mrs. Haller, you are a nimble walker: I should be sorry to run a race with you.

Mrs. H. Custom, my lord. You need only take the same walk every day for a month.

Count. Yes; if I wanted to resemble my greyhounds.—But what said the Stranger?

Countess. He gave Charlotte a flat refusal; and you see his door, and even his shutters, are closed against us.

Count. What an unaccountable being! But it won't do. I must show my gratitude one way or other. Steinfort, we will take the ladies home, and then you shall try once again to see him. You can talk to these oddities better than I can.

Bar. If you wish it, with all my heart.

Count. Thank you, thank you. Come, ladies: come Mrs. Haller.

[*Exeunt.*

SCENE II.

A close walk in the Garden.

Enter Countess, *and* Mrs. Haller.

Countess. Well, Mrs. Haller, how do you like the man that just now left us?

Mrs. H. Who?

Countess. My brother.

Mrs. H. He deserves to be your brother.

Countess. [*Curtseying.*] Your most obedient! That shall be written in my pocket-book.

Mrs. H. Without flattery then, madam, he appears to be most amiable.

Countess. Good!—And a handsome man?

Mrs. H. [*With indifference.*] Oh, yes.

Countess. "Oh, yes!" It sounded almost like, "Oh, no!" But I must tell you, that he looks upon you to be a handsome woman [Mrs. Haller *smiles.*] You make no reply to this?

Mrs. H. What shall I reply? Derision never fell from your lips; and I am little calculated to support it.

Countess. As little as you are calculated to be the cause of it. No; I was in earnest.—Now?

Mrs. H. You confuse me!—But why should I play the prude? I will own there was a time, when I thought myself handsome. 'Tis past. Alas! the enchanting beauties of a female countenance arise from peace of mind—The look, which captivates an honourable man, must be reflected from a noble soul.

Countess. Then Heaven grant my bosom may ever hold as pure a heart, as now those eyes bear witness lives in yours!

Mrs. H. [*With sudden wildness.*] Oh! Heaven forbid!

Countess. [*Astonished.*] How!

Mrs. H. [*Checking her tears.*] Spare me! I am a wretch. The sufferings of three years can give me no claim to your friendship— No, not even to your compassion. Oh! spare me!

[*Going.*

Countess. Stay, Mrs. Haller. For the first time, I beg your confidence.—My brother loves you.

Mrs. H. [*Starting, and gazing full in the face of the* Countess.] For mirth, too much—for earnest, too mournful!

Countess. I revere that modest blush. Discover to me who you are. You risk nothing. Pour all your griefs into a sister's bosom. Am I not kind? and can I not be silent?

Mrs. H. Alas! But a frank reliance on a generous mind is the greatest sacrifice to be offered by true repentance. This sacrifice I will offer. [*Hesitating.*] Did you never hear—Pardon me—Did you never hear—Oh! how shocking is it to unmask a deception, which alone has recommended me to your regard! But it must be so.—Madam—Fie, Adelaide! does pride become you? Did you never hear of the Countess Waldbourg?

Countess. I think I did hear, at the neighbouring court, of such a creature. She plunged an honourable husband into misery. She ran away with a villain.

Mrs. H. She did indeed. [*Falls at the feet of the* Countess.] Do not cast me from you.

Countess. For Heaven's sake! You are—

Mrs. H. I am that wretch.

Countess. [*Turning from her with horror.*] Ha!—Begone! [*Going. Her heart draws her back.*] Yet, she is unfortunate: she is unfriended! Her image is repentance—Her life the proof—She has wept her fault in her three years agony. Be still awhile, remorseless prejudice, and let the genuine feelings of my soul avow—they do not truly honour virtue, who can insult the erring heart that would return to her sanctuary. [*Looking with sorrow on her.*] Rise, I beseech you, rise! My husband and my brother may surprise us. I promise to be silent.

[*Raising her.*

Mrs. H. Yes, you will be silent—But, oh! conscience! conscience! thou never wilt be silent. [*Clasping her hands.*] Do not cast me from you.

Countess. Never! Your lonely life, your silent anguish and contrition, may at length atone your crime. And never shall you want an asylum, where your penitence may lament your loss. Your crime was youth and inexperience; your heart never was, never could be concerned in it.

Mrs. H. Oh! spare me! My conscience never martyrs me so horribly, as when I catch my base thoughts in search of an excuse! No, nothing can palliate my guilt; and the only just consolation left me, is, to acquit the man I wronged, and own I erred without a cause of fair complaint.

Countess. And this is the mark of true repentance. Alas! my friend, when superior sense, recommended too by superior charms of person, assail a young, though wedded—

Mrs. H. Ah! not even that mean excuse is left me. In all that merits admiration, respect, and love, he was far, far beneath my husband. But to attempt to account for my strange infatuation—I cannot bear it. I thought my husband's manner grew colder to me. 'Tis true I knew, that his expenses, and his confidence in deceitful friends, had embarrassed his means, and clouded his spirits; yet I thought he denied me pleasures and amusements still within our reach. My vanity was mortified! My confidence not courted. The serpent tongue of my seducer promised every thing. But never could such arguments avail, till, assisted by forged letters, and the treachery of a servant, whom I most confided in, he fixed my belief that my lord was false, and that all the coldness I complained of was disgust to me, and love for another; all his home retrenchments but the means of satisfying a rival's luxury. Maddened with this conviction, (conviction it was, for artifice was most ingenious in its proof,) I left my children—father—husband—to follow—a villain.

Countess. But, with such a heart, my friend could not remain long in her delusion?

Mrs. H. Long enough to make sufficient penitence impossible. 'Tis true that in a few weeks the delirium was at an end. Oh, what were my sensations when the mist dispersed before my eyes? I called for my husband, but in vain!—I listened for the prattle of my children, but in vain!

Countess. [*Embracing her.*] Here, here, on this bosom only shall your future tears be shed; and may I, dear sufferer, make you again familiar with hope!

Mrs. H. Oh! impossible!

Countess. Have you never heard of your children?

Mrs. H. Never.

Countess. We must endeavour to gain some account of them. We must—Hold! my husband and my brother! Oh, my poor brother! I had quite forgotten him. Quick, dear Mrs. Haller, wipe your eyes. Let us meet them.

Mrs. H. Madam, I'll follow. Allow me a moment to compose myself.—[*Exit* Countess.] I pause!—Oh! yes—to compose myself! [*Ironically.*] She little thinks it is but to gain one solitary moment to vent my soul's remorse. Once the purpose of my unsettled mind was self-destruction; Heaven knows how I have sued for hope and resignation. I did trust my prayers were heard—Oh! spare me further trial! I feel, I feel, my heart and brain can bear no more.

[*Exit.*

ACT THE FOURTH.

SCENE I.

The Skirts of the Park, Lodge, &c. as before.—A Table, spread with Fruits, &c.

Francis *discovered placing the supper.*

Fra. I know he loves to have his early supper in the fresh air; and, while he sups, not that I believe any thing can amuse him, yet I will try my little Savoyards' pretty voices. I have heard him speak as if he had loved music. [*Music without.*] Oh, here they are.

Enter Annette *and* Claudine, *playing on their guitars.*

Ann. *To welcome mirth and harmless glee, We rambling minstrels, blythe and free, With song the laughing hours beguile, And wear a never-fading smile: Where'er we roam We find a home, And greeting, to reward our toil.*

Clau. *No anxious griefs disturb our rest, Nor busy cares annoy our breast; Fearless we sink in soft repose, While night her sable mantle throws. With grateful lay, Hail rising day, That rosy health and peace bestows.*

During the Duet, the Stranger *looks from the Lodge window, and at the conclusion he comes out.*

Stra. What mummery is this?

Fra. I hoped it might amuse you, sir.

Stra. Amuse *me*—fool!

Fra. Well then, I wished to amuse myself a little. I don't think my recreations are so very numerous.

Stra. That's true, my poor fellow; indeed they are not. Let them go on.—I'll listen.

Fra. But to please you, poor master, I fear it must be a sadder strain. Annette, have you none but these cheerful songs?

Ann. O, plenty. If you are dolefully given we can be as sad as night. I'll sing you an air Mrs. Haller taught me the first year she came to the Castle.

Fra. Mrs. Haller! I should like to hear that.

Ann. *I have a silent sorrow here, A grief I'll ne'er impart; It breathes no sigh, it sheds no tear, But it consumes my heart; This cherish'd woe, this lov'd despair, My lot for ever be, So, my soul's lord, the pangs I bear Be never known by thee!*

And when pale characters of death Shall mark this alter'd cheek, When my poor wasted trembling breath My life's last hope would speak; I shall not raise my eyes to Heav'n, Nor mercy ask for me, My soul despairs to be forgiv'n, Unpardon'd, love, by thee.

Stra. [*Surprised and moved.*] Oh! I have heard that air before, but 'twas with other words. Francis, share our supper with your friends—I need none.

[*Enters the Lodge.*

Fra. So I feared. Well, my pretty favourites, here are refreshments. So, disturbed again. Now will this gentleman call for more music, and make my master mad. Return when you observe this man is gone.—[*Exeunt* Annette *and* Claudine.—Francis *sits and eats.*]—I was in hopes, that I might at least eat my supper peaceably in the open air; but they follow at our heels like blood-hounds.

Enter Baron.

Bar. My good friend, I must speak to your master.

Fra. Can't serve you.

Bar. Why not?

Fra. It's forbidden.

Bar. [*Offers money.*] There! announce me.

Fra. Want no money.

Bar. Well, only announce me then.

Fra. I will announce you, sir; but it won't avail! I shall be abused, and you rejected. However, we can but try.

[*Going.*

Bar. I only ask half a minute. [Francis *goes into the Lodge.*] But when he comes, how am I to treat him? I never encountered a misanthrope before. I have heard of instructions as to conduct in society; but how I am to behave towards a being who loathes the whole world, and his own existence, I have never learned.

Enter the Stranger.

Stra. Now; what's your will?

Bar. I beg pardon, sir, for—[*Suddenly recognizing him.*] Charles!

Stra. Steinfort!

[*They embrace.*

Bar. Is it really you, my dear friend?

Stra. It is.

Bar. Merciful Heavens! How you are altered!

Stra. The hand of misery lies heavy on me.—But how came you here? What want you?

Bar. Strange! Here was I ruminating how to address this mysterious recluse: he appears, and proves to be my old and dearest friend.

Stra. Then you were not in search of me, nor knew that I lived here?

Bar. As little as I know who lives on the summit of Caucasus. You this morning saved the life of my brother-in-law's only son: a grateful family wishes to behold you in its circle. You refused my sister's messenger; therefore, to give more weight to the invitation, I was deputed to be the bearer of it. And thus has fortune restored to me a friend, whom my heart has so long missed, and whom my heart just now so much requires.

Stra. Yes, I am your friend; your sincere friend. You are a true man; an uncommon man. Towards you my heart is still the same. But if this assurance be of any value to you—go—leave me—and return no more.

Bar. Stay! All that I see and hear of you is inexplicable. 'Tis you; but these, alas! are not the features which once enchanted every female bosom, beamed gaiety through all society, and won you friends before your lips were opened! Why do you avert your face? Is the sight of a friend become hateful? Or, do you fear, that I should read in your eye what passes in your soul? Where is that open look of fire, which at once penetrated into every heart, and revealed your own?

Stra. [*With asperity.*] My look penetrate into every heart!—Ha! ha! ha!

Bar. Oh, Heavens! Rather may I never hear you laugh than in such a tone!—For Heaven's sake tell me, Charles! tell me, I conjure you, what has happened to you?

Stra. Things that happen every day; occurrences heard of in every street. Steinfort, if I am not to hate you, ask me not another question. If I am to love you, leave me.

Bar. Oh, Charles! awake the faded ideas of past joys. Feel, that a friend is near. Recollect the days we passed in Hungary, when we wandered arm in arm upon the banks of the Danube, while nature opened our hearts, and made us enamoured of benevolence and friendship. In those blessed moments you gave me this seal as a pledge of your regard. Do you remember it?

Stra. Yes.

Bar. Am I since that time become less worthy of your confidence?

Stra. No!

Bar. Charles! it grieves me that I am thus compelled to enforce my rights upon you. Do you know this scar?

Stra. Comrade! Friend! It received and resisted the stroke aimed at my life. I have not forgotten it. Alas! you knew not what a present you then made me.

Bar. Speak then, I beseech you.

Stra. You cannot help me.

Bar. Then I can mourn with you.

Stra. That I hate. Besides, I cannot weep.

Bar. Then give me words instead of tears. Both relieve the heart.

Stra. Relieve the heart! My heart is like a close-shut sepulchre. Let what is within it, moulder and decay.—Why, why open the wretched charnel-house to spread a pestilence around?

Bar. How horrid are your looks! For shame! A man like you thus to crouch beneath the chance of fortune!

Stra. Steinfort! I did think, that the opinion of all mankind was alike indifferent to me; but I feel that it is not so. My friend, you shall not quit me without learning how I have been robbed of every joy which life afforded. Listen: much misery may be contained in a few words. Attracted by my native country, I quitted you and the service. What pleasing pictures did I draw of a life employed in improving society, and diffusing happiness! I fixed on Cassel to be my abode. All went on admirably. I found friends. At length, too, I found a wife; a lovely, innocent creature, scarce sixteen years of age. Oh! how I loved her! She bore me a son and a daughter. Both were endowed by nature with the beauty of their mother. Ask me not how I loved my wife and children! Yes, then, then I was really happy. [*Wiping his eyes.*] Ha! a tear! I could not have believed it. Welcome, old friends! 'Tis long since we have known each other. Well, my story is nearly ended. One of my friends, for whom I had become engaged, treacherously lost me more than half my fortune. This hurt me. I was obliged to retrench my expenses. Contentment needs but little. I forgave him. Another friend—a villain! to whom I was attached heart and soul; whom I had assisted with my means, and promoted by my interest, this fiend! seduced my wife, and bore her from me. Tell me, sir, is this enough to justify my hatred of mankind, and palliate my seclusion from the world?—Kings—laws—tyranny—or guilt can but imprison me, or kill me. But, O God! O God! Oh! what are chains or death compared to the tortures of a deceived yet doting husband!

Bar. To lament the loss of a faithless wife is madness.

Stra. Call it what you please—say what you please—I love her still.

Bar. And where is she?

Stra. I know not, nor do I wish to know.

Bar. And your children?

Stra. I left them at a small town hard by.

Bar. But why did you not keep your children with you? They would have amused you in many a dreary hour.

Stra. Amused me! Oh, yes! while their likeness to their mother would every hour remind me of my past happiness! No. For three years I have never seen them. I hate that any human creature should be near me, young or old! Had not ridiculous habits made a servant necessary, I should long since have discharged him; though he is not the worst among the bad.

Bar. Such too often are the consequences of great alliances. Therefore, Charles, I have resolved to take a wife from a lower rank of life.

Stra. You marry!—Ha! ha! ha!

Bar. You shall see her. She is in the house where you are expected. Come with me.

Stra. What! I mix again with the world!

Bar. To do a generous action without requiring thanks is noble and praise-worthy. But so obstinately to avoid those thanks, as to make the kindness a burden, is affectation.

Stra. Leave me! leave me! Every one tries to form a circle, of which he may be the centre. As long as there remains a bird in these woods to greet the rising sun with its melody, I shall court no other society.

Bar. Do as you please to-morrow; but give me your company this evening.

Stra. [*Resolutely.*] No!

Bar. Not though it were in your power, by this single visit, to secure the happiness of your friend for life?

Stra. [*Starting.*] Ha! then I must—But how?—

Bar. You shall sue in my behalf to Mrs. Haller—You have the talent of persuasion.

Stra. I! my dear Steinfort!

Bar. The happiness or misery of your friend depends upon it. I'll contrive that you shall speak to her alone. Will you?

Stra. I will; but upon one condition.

Bar. Name it.

Stra. That you allow me to be gone to-morrow, and not endeavour to detain me.

Bar. Go! Whither?

Stra. No matter! Promise this, or I will not come.

Bar. Well, I do promise. Come.

Stra. I have directions to give my servant.

Bar. In half an hour then we shall expect you. Remember, you have given your word.

Stra. I have. [*Exit* Baron.—*The* Stranger *walks up and down, thoughtful and melancholy.*]—Francis!

Enter Francis.

Fra. Sir!

Stra. Why are you out of the way?

Fran. Sir, I came when I heard you call.

Stra. I shall leave this place to-morrow.

Fra. With all my heart.

Stra. Perhaps to go into another land.

Fra. With all my heart again.

Stra. Perhaps into another quarter of the globe.

Fra. With all my heart still. Into which quarter?

Stra. Wherever Heaven directs! Away! away! from Europe! From this cultivated moral lazaret! Do you hear, Francis? To-morrow early.

Fra. Very well.

[*Going.*

Stra. Come here, come here first, I have an errand for you. Hire that carriage in the village; drive to the town hard by; you may be back by sun-set. I shall give you a letter to a widow who lives there. With her you will find two children. They are mine.

Fra. [*Astonished.*] Your children, sir!

Stra. Take them, and bring them hither.

Fra. Your children, sir!

Stra. Yes, mine! Is it so very inconceivable?

Fra. That I should have been three years in your service, and never have heard them mentioned, is somewhat strange.

Stra. Pshaw!

Fra. You have been married then?

Stra. Go, and prepare for our journey.

Fra. That I can do in five minutes.

[*Going.*

Stra. I shall come and write the letter directly.

Fra. Very well, sir.

[*Exit.*

Stra. Yes, I'll take them with me. I'll accustom myself to the sight of them. The innocents! they shall not be poisoned by the refinements of society. Rather let them hunt their daily sustenance upon some desert island with their bow and arrow; or creep, like torpid Hottentots, into a corner, and stare at each other. Better to do nothing than to do evil. Fool that I was, to be prevailed upon once more to exhibit myself among these apes! What a ridiculous figure shall I be! and in the capacity of a suitor too! Pshaw! he cannot be serious! 'Tis but a friendly artifice to draw me from my solitude. Why did I promise him? Yes, my sufferings have been many; and, to oblige a friend, why should I hesitate to add another painful hour to the wretched calendar of my life! I'll go. I'll go.

[*Exit.*

SCENE II.

The Antichamber.

Enter Charlotte.

Char. No, indeed, my lady! If you chuse to bury yourself in the country, I shall take my leave. I am not calculated for a country life. And, to sum up all, when I think of this Mrs. Haller—

Enter Solomon.

Sol. [*Overhearing her last words.*] What of Mrs. Haller, my sweet Miss?

Char. Why, Mr. Solomon, who is Mrs. Haller? You know every thing; you hear every thing.

Sol. I have received no letters from any part of Europe on the subject, Miss.

Char. But who is to blame? The Count and Countess. She dines with them; and at this very moment is drinking tea with them. Is this proper?

Sol. By no means.

Char. Shouldn't a Count and a Countess, in all their actions, show a certain degree of pride and pomposity?

Sol. To be sure! To be sure they should!

Char. No, I won't submit to it. I'll tell her ladyship, when I dress her to-morrow, that either Mrs. Haller or I must quit the house.

Sol. [*Seeing the* Baron.] St!

Enter Baron.

Bar. Didn't I hear Mrs. Haller's name here?

Sol. [*Confused.*] Why—yes—we—we—

Bar. Charlotte, tell my sister I wish to see her as soon as the tea-table is removed.

Char. [*Aside to* Solomon.] Either she or I go, that I'm determined.

[*Exit.*

Bar. May I ask what it was you were saying?

Sol. Why, please your Honourable Lordship, we were talking here and there—this and that—

Bar. I almost begin to suspect some secret.

Sol. Secret! Heaven forbid! Mercy on us! No! I should have had letters on the subject if there had been a secret.

Bar. Well then, since it was no secret, I presume I may know your conversation.

Sol. You do us great honour, my lord. Why, then, at first, we were making a few common-place observations. Miss Charlotte remarked that we had all our faults. I said, "Yes." Soon after I remarked that the best persons in the world were not without their weaknesses. She said, "Yes."

Bar. If you referred to Mrs. Haller's faults and weaknesses, I am desirous to hear more.

Sol. Sure enough, sir, Mrs. Haller is an excellent woman; but she's not an angel for all that. I am an old faithful servant to his Excellency the Count, and therefore it is my duty to speak, when any thing is done disadvantageous to his interest.

Bar. Well!

Sol. For instance, now; his Excellency may think he has at least some score of dozens of the old six-and-twenty hock. Mercy on us!

there are not ten dozen bottles left; and not a drop has gone down my throat, I'll swear.

Bar. [*Smiling.*] Mrs. Haller has not drank it, I suppose?

Sol. Not she herself, for she never drinks wine. But if any body be ill in the village, any poor woman lying-in, away goes a bottle of the six-and-twenty! Innumerable are the times that I've reproved her; but she always answers me snappishly, that she will be responsible for it.

Bar. So will I, Mr. Solomon.

Sol. Oh! with all my heart, your Honourable Lordship. It makes no difference to me. I had the care of the cellar twenty years, and can safely take my oath, that I never gave the poor a single drop in the whole course of my trust.

Bar. How extraordinary is this woman!

Sol. Extraordinary! One can make nothing of her. To-day, the vicar's wife is not good enough for her. To-morrow, you may see her sitting with all the women of the village. To be sure she and I agree pretty well; for, between me and your Honourable Lordship, she has cast an eye upon my son Peter.

Bar. Has she?

Sol. Yes—Peter's no fool, I assure you. The schoolmaster is teaching him to write. Would your Honourable Lordship please to see a specimen; I'll go for his copy-book. He makes his pothooks capitally.

Bar. Another time, another time. Good bye for the present, Mr. Solomon. [Solomon *bows, without attempting to go.*] Good day, Mr. Solomon.

Sol. [*Not understanding the hint.*] Your Honourable Lordship's most obedient servant.

Bar. Mr. Solomon I wish to be alone.

Sol. As your lordship commands. If the time should seem long in my absence, and your lordship wishes to hear the newest news from the seat of war, you need only send for old Solomon. I have letters from Leghorn, Cape Horn, and every known part of the habitable globe.

[*Exit.*

Bar. Tedious old fool! Yet hold. Did he not speak in praise of Mrs. Haller? Pardoned be his rage for news and politics.

Enter Countess.

Well, sister, have you spoken to her?

Countess. I have: and if you do not steer for another haven, you will be doomed to drive upon the ocean for ever.

Bar. Is she married?

Countess. I don't know.

Bar. Is she of a good family?

Countess. I can't tell.

Bar. Does she dislike me?

Countess. Excuse my making a reply.

Bar. I thank you for your sisterly affection, and the explicitness of your communications. Luckily, I placed little reliance on either;

and have found a friend, who will save your ladyship all further trouble.

Countess. A friend!

Bar. Yes. The Stranger who saved your son's life this morning proves to be my intimate friend.

Countess. What's his name?

Bar. I don't know.

Countess. Is he of a good family?

Bar. I can't tell.

Countess. Will he come hither?

Bar. Excuse my making a reply.

Countess. Well, the retort is fair—but insufferable.

Bar. You can't object to the *Da Capo* of your own composition,

Enter Count *and* Mrs. Haller.

Count. Zounds! do you think I am Xenocrates; or like the poor sultan with marble legs? There you leave me *tête-a-tête* with Mrs. Haller, as if my heart were a mere flint. So you prevailed, brother. The Stranger will come then, it seems.

Bar. I expect him every minute.

Count. I'm glad to hear it. One companion more, however. In the country we never can have too many.

Bar. This gentleman will not exactly be an addition to your circle, for he leaves this place tomorrow.

Count. But he won't, I think. Now, Lady Wintersen, summon all your charms. There is no art in conquering us poor devils; but this strange man, who does not care a doit for you all together, is worth your efforts. Try your skill. I shan't be jealous.

Countess. I allow the conquest to be worth the trouble. But what Mrs. Haller has not been able to affect in three months, ought not to be attempted by me.

Mrs. H. [*Jocosely.*] Oh, yes, madam. He has given me no opportunity of trying the force of my charms, for I have never once happened to see him.

Count. Then he's a blockhead; and you an idler.

Sol. [*Without.*] This way, sir! This way!

Enter Solomon.

Sol. The Stranger begs leave to have the honour—

Count. Welcome! Welcome.

[*Exit* Solomon.

[*Turns to meet the* Stranger, *whom he conducts in by the hand.*]

My dear sir—Lady Wintersen—Mrs. Haller—

[Mrs. Haller, *as soon as she sees the* Stranger, *shrieks, and swoons in the arms of the* Baron. *The* Stranger *casts a look at her, and struck with astonishment and horror, rushes out of the room. The* Baron *and* Countess *bear* Mrs. Haller *off;* Count *following, in great surprise.*]

ACT THE FIFTH.

SCENE I.

The Antichamber.

Enter Baron.

Bar. Oh! deceitful hope! Thou phantom of future happiness! To thee have I stretched out my arms, and thou hast vanished into air! Wretched Steinfort! The mystery is solved. She is the wife of my friend! I cannot myself be happy; but I may, perhaps, be able to reunite two lovely souls, whom cruel fate has severed. Ha! they are here. I must propose it instantly.

Enter Countess *and* Mrs. Haller.

Countess. Into the garden, my dear friend! Into the air!

Mrs. H. I am quite well. Do not alarm yourselves on my account.

Bar. Madam, pardon my intrusion; but to lose a moment may be fatal. He means to quit the country to-morrow. We must devise means to reconcile you to—the Stranger.

Mrs. H. How, my lord! You seem acquainted with my history?

Bar. I am. Walbourg has been my friend ever since we were boys. We served together from the rank of cadet. We have been separated seven years. Chance brought us this day together, and his heart was open to me.

Mrs. H. Now do I feel what it is to be in the presence of an honest man, when I dare not meet his eye.

[*Hides her face.*

Bar. If sincere repentance, if years without reproach, do not give us a title to man's forgiveness, what must we expect hereafter? No, lovely penitent! your contrition is complete. Error for a moment wrested from slumbering virtue the dominion of your heart; but she awoke, and, with a look, banished her enemy for ever. I know my friend. He has the firmness of a man; but, with it, the gentlest feelings of your sex. I hasten to him. With the fire of pure disinterested friendship will I enter on this work; that, when I look back upon my past life, I may derive from this good action consolation in disappointment, and even resignation in despair.

[*Going.*

Mrs. H. Oh, stay! What would you do? No! never! My husband's honour is sacred to me. I love him unutterably: but never, never can I be his wife again; even if he were generous enough to pardon me.

Bar. Madam! Can you, Countess, be serious?

Mrs H. Not that title, I beseech you! I am not a child, who wishes to avoid deserved punishment. What were my penitence, if I hoped advantage from it beyond the consciousness of atonement for past offence?

Countess. But if your husband himself—?

Mrs. H. Oh! he will not! he cannot! And let him rest assured I never would replace my honour at the expense of his.

Bar. He still loves you.

Mrs. H. Loves me! Then he must not—No—he must purify his heart from a weakness which would degrade him!

Bar. Incomparable woman! I go to my friend—perhaps, for the last time! Have you not one word to send him?

Mrs. H. Yes, I have two requests to make. Often when, in excess of grief, I have despaired of every consolation, I have thought I should be easier if I might behold my husband once again, acknowledge my injustice to him, and take a gentle leave of him for ever. This, therefore, is my first request—a conversation for a few short minutes, if he does not quite abhor the sight of me. My second request is—Oh—not to see, but to hear some account of my poor children.

Bar. If humanity and friendship can avail, he will not for a moment delay your wishes.

Countess. Heaven be with you.

Mrs. H. And my prayers.

[*Exit* Baron.

Countess. Come, my friend, come into the air, till he returns with hope and consolation.

Mrs. H. Oh, my heart! How art thou afflicted! My husband! My little ones! Past joys and future fears—Oh, dearest madam, there are moments in which we live years! Moments, which steal the roses from the cheek of health, and plough deep furrows in the brow of youth.

Countess. Banish these sad reflections. Come, let us walk. The sun will set soon; let nature's beauties dissipate anxiety.

Mrs. H. Alas! Yes, the setting sun is a proper scene for me.

Countess. Never forget a morning will succeed.

[*Exeunt.*

SCENE II.

The skirts of the Park, Lodge, &c. as before.

Enter Baron.

Bar. On earth there is but one such pair. They shall not be parted. Yet what I have undertaken is not so easy as I at first hoped. What can I answer when he asks me, whether I would persuade him to renounce his character, and become the derision of society? For he is right: a faithless wife is a dishonour! and to forgive her, is to share her shame. What though Adelaide may be an exception; a young deluded girl, who has so long and so sincerely repented, yet what cares an unfeeling world for this? The world! he has quitted it. 'Tis evident he loves her still; and upon this assurance builds my sanguine heart the hope of a happy termination to an honest enterprise.

Enter Francis *with two Children,* William *and* Amelia.

Fra. Come along, my pretty ones—come.

Will. Is it far to home?

Fra. No, we shall be there directly, now.

Bar. Hold! Whose children are these?

Fra. My master's.

Will. Is that my father?

Bar. It darts like lightning through my brain. A word with you. I know you love your master. Strange things have happened here. Your master has found his wife again.

Fra. Indeed! Glad to hear it.

Bar. Mrs. Haller—

Fra. Is she his wife? Still more glad to hear it.

Bar. But he is determined to go from her.

Fra. Oh!

Bar. We must try to prevent it.

Fra. Surely.

Bar. The unexpected appearance of the children may perhaps assist us.

Fra. How so?

Bar. Hide yourself with them in that hut. Before a quarter of an hour is passed you shall know more.

Fra. But—

Bar. No more questions, I entreat you. Time is precious.

Fra. Well, well: questions are not much in my way. Come, children.

Will. Why, I thought you told me I should see my father.

Fra. So you shall, my dear. Come, moppets.

[*Goes into the Hut with the Children.*

Bar. Excellent! I promise myself much from this little artifice. If the mild look of the mother fails, the innocent smiles of these his own children will surely find the way to his heart. [*Taps at the Lodge door, the* Stranger *comes out.*] Charles, I wish you joy.

Stra. Of what?

Bar. You have found her again.

Stra. Show a bankrupt the treasure which he once possessed, and then congratulate him on the amount!

Bar. Why not, if it be in your power to retrieve the whole?

Stra. I understand you: you are a negociator from my wife. It won't avail.

Bar. Learn to know your wife better. Yes, I am a messenger from her; but without power to treat. She, who loves you unutterably, who without you never can be happy, renounces your forgiveness; because, as she thinks, your honour is incompatible with such a weakness.

Stra. Pshaw! I am not to be caught.

Bar. Charles! consider well—

Stra. Steinfort, let me explain all this. I have lived here four months. Adelaide knew it.

Bar. Knew it! She never saw you till to-day.

Stra. That you may make fools believe. Hear further: she knows too, that I am not a common sort of man; that my heart is not to be attacked in the usual way. She, therefore, framed a deep concerted plan. She played a charitable part; but in such a way, that it always reached my ears. She played a pious, modest, reserved part, in order to excite my curiosity. And at last, to-day she plays the prude. She refuses my forgiveness, in hopes by this generous device, to extort it from my compassion.

Bar. Charles! I have listened to you with astonishment. This is a weakness only to be pardoned in a man who has so often been deceived by the world. Your wife has expressly and stedfastly declared, that she will not accept your forgiveness, even if you yourself were weak enough to offer it.

Stra. What then has brought you hither?

Bar. More than one reason. First, I am come in my own name, as your friend and comrade, to conjure you solemnly not to spurn this creature from you; for, by my soul, you will not find her equal.

Stra. Give yourself no further trouble.

Bar. Be candid, Charles. You love her still.

Stra. Alas! yes.

Bar. Her sincere repentance has long since obliterated her crime.

Stra. Sir! a wife, once induced to forfeit her honour, must be capable of a second crime.

Bar. Not so, Charles. Ask your heart what portion of the blame may be your own.

Stra. Mine!

Bar. Yours. Who told you to marry a thoughtless inexperienced girl? One scarce expects established principles at five-and-twenty in a man, yet you require them in a girl of sixteen! But of this no more. She has erred; she has repented; and, during three years, her conduct has been so far above reproach, that even the piercing eye of calumny has not discovered a speck upon this radiant orb.

Stra. Now, were I to believe all this—and I confess that I would willingly believe it—yet can she never again be mine. [*With extreme asperity.*] Oh! what a feast would it be for the painted dolls and vermin of the world, when I appeared among them with my runaway wife upon my arm! What mocking, whispering, pointing!—Never! Never! Never!

Bar. Enough! As a friend I have done my duty: I now appear as Adelaide's ambassador. She requests one moment's conversation. She wishes once again to see you, and never more! You cannot deny her this, this only, this last, request.

Stra. Oh! I understand this too: she thinks my firmness will be melted by her tears: she is mistaken. She may come.

Bar. She will come, to make you feel how much you mistake her. I go for her.

Stra. Another word.

Bar. Another word!

Stra. Give her this paper, and these jewels. They belong to her.

[*Presenting them.*

Bar. That you may do yourself.

[*Exit.*

Stra. The last anxious moment of my life draws near. I shall see her once again; I shall see her, on whom my soul doats. Is this the language of an injured husband? What is this principle which we call honour? Is it a feeling of the heart, or a quibble in the brain? I must be resolute: it cannot now be otherwise. Let me speak solemnly, yet mildly; and beware that nothing of reproach escape my lips. Yes, her penitence is real. She shall not be obliged to live in mean dependence: she shall be mistress of herself, she shall— [*Looks round and shudders.*] Ha! they come. Awake, insulted pride! Protect me, injured honour!

Enter Mrs. Haller, Countess, *and* Baron.

Mrs. H. [*Advances slowly, and in a tremour.* Countess *attempts to support her.*] Leave me now, I beseech you. [*Approaches the*

Stranger, *who, with averted countenance, and in extreme agitation, awaits her address.*] My lord!

Stra. [*With gentle tremulous utterance, and face still turned away.*] What would you with me, Adelaide?

Mrs. H. [*Much agitated.*] No—for Heaven's sake! I was not prepared for this—Adelaide!—No, no. For Heaven's sake!—Harsh tones alone are suited to a culprit's ear.

Stra. [*Endeavouring to give his voice firmness.*] Well, madam!

Mrs. H. Oh! if you will ease my heart, if you will spare and pity me, use reproaches.

Stra. Reproaches! Here they are; here on my sallow cheek—here in my hollow eye—here in my faded form. These reproaches I could not spare you.

Mrs. H. Were I a hardened sinner, this forbearance would be charity: but I am a suffering penitent, and it overpowers me. Alas! then I must be the herald of my own shame. For, where shall I find peace, till I have eased my soul by my confession?

Stra. No confession, madam. I release you from every humiliation. I perceive you feel, that we must part for ever.

Mrs. H. I know it. Nor come I here to supplicate your pardon; nor has my heart contained a ray of hope that you would grant it. All I dare ask is, that you will not curse my memory.

Stra. [*Moved.*] No, I do not curse you. I shall never curse you.

Mrs. H. [*Agitated.*] From the conviction that I am unworthy of your name, I have, during three years abandoned it. But this is not enough; you must have that redress which will enable you to chuse another—another wife; in whose chaste arms, may Heaven protect your hours in bliss! This paper will be necessary for the purpose: it contains a written acknowledgement of my guilt.

[*Offers it, trembling.*

Stra. [*Tearing it.*] Perish the record, for ever.—No, Adelaide, you only have possessed my heart; and, I am not ashamed to own it, you alone will reign there for ever.—Your own sensations of virtue, your resolute honour, forbid you to profit by my weakness; and even if—Now, by Heaven, this is beneath a man! But—never—never will another fill Adelaide's place here.

Mrs. H. [*Trembling.*] Then nothing now remains but that one sad, hard, just word—farewell!

Stra. Stay a moment. For some months we have, without knowing it, lived near each other. I have learnt much good of you. You have a heart open to the wants of your fellow creatures. I am happy that it is so. You shall not be without the power of gratifying your benevolence. I know you have a spirit that must shrink from a state of obligation. This paper, to which the whole remnant of my fortune is pledged, secures you independence, Adelaide: and let the only recommendation of the gift be, that it will administer to you the means of indulging in charity, the divine propensity of your nature.

Mrs. H. Never! To the labour of my hands alone will I owe my sustenance. A morsel of bread, moistened with the tear of penitence, will suffice my wishes, and exceed my merits. It would be an additional reproach, to think that I served myself, or even others, from the bounty of the man whom I had so deeply injured.

Stra. Take it, madam; take it.

Mrs. H. I have deserved this. But I throw myself upon your generosity. Have compassion on me!

Stra. [*Aside.*] Villain! of what a woman hast thou robbed me!—[*Puts up the paper.*] Well, madam, I respect your sentiments, and withdraw my request; but on condition, that if you ever should be in want of any thing, I may be the first and only person in the world, to whom you will make application.

Mrs. H. I promise it, my lord.

Stra. And now I may, at least, desire you to take back what is your own—your jewels.

[*Gives her the casket.*

Mrs. H. [*Opens it in violent agitation, and her tears burst upon it.*] How well do I recollect the sweet evening when you gave me these! That evening, my father joined our hands; and joyfully I pronounced the oath of eternal fidelity.—It is broken. This locket, you gave me on my birthday—That was a happy day! We had a country feast—How cheerful we all were!—This bracelet, I received after my William was born! No! take them—take them—I cannot keep these, unless you wish, that the sight of them should be an incessant reproach to my almost broken heart.

[*Gives them back.*

Stra. [*Aside.*] I must go. My soul and pride will hold no longer. [*Turning towards her.*] Farewell!—

Mrs. H. Oh! but one minute more! An answer to but one more question,—Feel for a mother's heart!—Are my children still alive?

Stra. Yes, they are alive.

Mrs. H. And well?

Stra. Yes, they are well.

Mrs. H. Heaven be praised! William must be much grown?

Stra. I believe so.

Mrs. H. What! have you not seen them!—And little Amelia, is she still your favourite? [*The* Stranger, *who is in violent agitation throughout this scene, remains in silent contention between honour and affection.*] Oh! let me behold them once again!—let me once more kiss the features of their father in his babes, and I will kneel to you, and part with them for ever.

[*She kneels—he raises her.*

Stra. Willingly, Adelaide! This very night. I expect the children every minute. They have been brought up near this spot. I have already sent my servant for them. He might, ere this time, have returned. I pledge my word to send them to the Castle as soon as they arrive. There, if you please, they may remain 'till daybreak to-morrow: then they must go with me.

[*The* Countess *and* Baron, *who at a little distance have listened to the whole conversation with the warmest sympathy, exchange signals.* Baron *goes into the Hut, and soon returns with* Francis *and the* Children. *He gives the* Girl *to the* Countess, *who places herself behind the* Stranger. *He himself walks with the* Boy *behind* Mrs. Haller.

Mrs. H. In this world, then—We have no more to say—— [*Seizing his hand.*] Forget a wretch, who never will forget you.—And when my penance shall have broken my heart,—when we again meet, in a better world——

Stra. There, Adelaide, you may be mine again.

H. }

}Oh! Oh! [*Parting.*

}

[*But, as they are going, she encounters the* Boy, *and he the* Girl.

80

Children. Dear father! Dear mother!

[*They press the* Children *in their arms with speechless affection; then tear themselves away—gaze at each other—spread their arms, and rush into an embrace. The* Children *run, and cling round their Parents. The curtain falls.*

Printed in Great Britain
by Amazon